# Lizzy the Pizzly

Written by Meghan DesLauriers

Illustrated by Amanda Letcher

Illustrations and design by Amanda Letcher

ISBN: 979-8-9910016-0-1 (paperback)
ISBN: 979-8-9910016-1-8 (hardcover)

First edition 2024
Published by Lind & Lo Books, LLC
Edina, Minnesota
meghandeslauriers.com

For Jane Elizabeth and Kathryn Grace

Lizzy was a pizzly bear,
the rarest of the rare.

Her mama was a grizzly,

and her pop a polar bear.

With heaps of frizzy, fuzzy fur

and eyes that dazzled blue,

**big** paws and claws

and **giant** jaws,

and husky shoulders, too.

Yes, Lizzy was a pizzly bear,
a scarce, peculiar breed.
The one and only pizzly
that she'd ever known or seen.

Now, Lizzy wasn't frazzled
by the fact that she was strange.
She thrived on being different
and she didn't want to change.

But on those drizzly, drabby days
when things were not-so-great,
young Lizzy dreamed of pizzly pals -
true friends who could relate.

And so, one day she grabbed a map
and set off on a quest

to find another pizzly bear,
a friend unlike the rest.

A few skips down her pizzly path,
the wind began to whir,
and Lizzy eyed a beast-like thing
with frizzy, fuzzy fur.

"Oh tizz! Oh fizz! Oh mizz! Oh my!
Is that a pizzly bear I spy?"

But as the beast came into view,
it looked more like a sheep,
all jumbled up with billy goat -
turns out it was a . . .

# GEEP!

"Oh, YOU are not a pizzly bear!"
"I'm not," the geep confessed.

"I've seen one though, not long ago,
I saw him headed west."

And then the frizzy, fuzzy geep
proposed a noble plan:
"May I come walk beside you
as a friendly, helping hand?"

Well, Lizzy beamed and said, "Indeed!"
then shared her pizzly name.

And just like that, the two were pals.
Both different yet the same.

The two looked high,
they looked down low,
they searched the forest through,

until they saw an animal
with eyes that dazzled blue.

"Oh tizz! Oh fizz! Oh mizz! Oh my!
Is that a pizzly bear I spy?"

But as the shape came into view,
it looked more like a horse,
half zebra-striped with black and white,
of course, it was a . . .

# ZORSE!

"Oh, YOU are not a pizzly bear!"
"No, ma'am," the zorse replied.
"I've seen one though, not long ago,
may I serve as a guide?"

Well, Lizzy beamed and said, "Indeed!"
then shared her pizzly name.
And just like that, the two were pals.

Both different yet the same.

And thus the three became a team,
united in a scheme
to find the other pizzly bear,
the friend in Lizzy's dream.

But as they searched (and laughed and sang),
sweet Lizzy felt at ease.
Turns out she didn't need a pizz...

"Wait! What's behind those trees?!"

"Oh tizz! Oh fizz! Oh mizz! Oh my!
That IS a pizzly bear I spy!"

"Yes, that's him! The pizzly bear!"
the geep and zorse both cried.

"With paws and claws and giant jaws
and shoulders extra wide!"

But then the bear surprised them all
and tilted his soft head.
"A pizzly bear? That isn't right.

# A GROLAR bear!" he said.

"Yes, I'm a solo grolar bear,
the rarest of the rare.
My papa was a grizzly
and my mom a polar bear."

"So you are not a pizzly bear?"
"Not quite," he gently said,
"but could you ever settle for
a grolar bear instead?"

Well, Lizzy beamed and said, "Indeed!"
then shared her pizzly name.
And just like that, the four were pals.

All different yet the same.

Milton Keynes UK
Ingram Content Group UK Ltd.
UKHW050753151024
449462UK00021B/51